DATE DUE

GAYLORD   PRINTED IN U.S.A

D1122567

Art by CHRISTIAN ZANIER and ANDREW PEPOY
Colors by DAVE STEWART

ANGEL

PAST LIVES

based on the television series created by

JOSS WHEDON & DAVID GREENWALT

writers CHRISTOPHER GOLDEN & TOM SNIEGOSKI

pencillers CHRISTIAN ZANIER & CLIFF RICHARDS

inkers JOE PIMENTEL & DIGITAL JUMP

colorist LEE LOUGHRIDGE *letterer* CLEM ROBINS *cover art* KEITH WOOD

dark horse comics®

publisher
MIKE RICHARDSON

editor
SCOTT ALLIE
WITH MICHAEL CARRIGLITTO

collection designer
KEITH WOOD

art director
MARK COX

Alexa Landry and various demons designed by
CHRISTIAN ZANIER

special thanks to
DEBBIE OLSHAN AT FOX LICENSING,
CAROLINE KALLAS AND GEORGE SNYDER AT *BUFFY THE VAMPIRE SLAYER*

PUBLISHED BY
DARK HORSE COMICS, INC.
10956 SE MAIN STREET
MILWAUKIE, OR 97222

FIRST EDITION
JULY 2001
ISBN: 1 - 56971 - 552 - 1

1 3 5 7 9 10 8 6 4 2

PRINTED IN SINGAPORE

Introduction

It had to be big.

On television, when *Buffy the Vampire Slayer* and *Angel* cross over, the producers have to coordinate not one but two armies of people, as well as storylines, and actors' schedules.

We didn't have to do that.

From the very start, we needed to take advantage of the fact that while, as a general rule, the show might have Buffy come to L.A., or Angel go to Sunnydale, or maybe Oz appear in *Angel* . . . we could do a lot more. We could bring the entire Scooby Gang to Los Angeles, to mix with Angel and Cordelia and Wesley for the first time since those characters had been spun off from the original series into its spawn.

So . . . we had that going for us. But, honestly, it wasn't going to be enough. As I said, if we were going to bother doing this thing at all, it had to be bigger than that. Certainly anytime you put Buffy and Angel in a room together, their past resonates in their every interaction. Bringing Giles in helps also, because, let's not forget, once upon a time Angel murdered his girlfriend and mercilessly tortured him. In truth, you could pick almost any combination of characters from these two series, put them together, and come up with a fascinating dynamic.

But all of that is sub-plot, theme, character. Wonderful stuff, but what about the plot?

The only thing Tom Sniegoski and I knew as we set out was that we wanted the story to take place in L.A. rather than Sunnydale, because, let's face it, that was more fun. More than likely, Angel wasn't going to call Buffy for help even if he was staked out like Gulliver on the beach and the sun was rising. Which meant that Angel had to be in some serious trouble, and Cordelia and Wesley had to be so outmatched that their only choice was to call Buffy.

Hmmm. Someone's gotta open up a serious can of whupass on Angel. That could be fun.

Still, though, not much of a story. So why don't I let you in on a little secret. Tom and I love Giles. His character is rich with potential, and yet so horribly underused, that we wanted to include him. Once we started to talk about that, ideas began to flow. Questions began to arise.

What's The Council of Watchers been up to since Buffy sent them packing? How have they dealt with what must be quite an embarrassment in the international supernatural espionage community?

What if the hunter who is after Angel also has ties to Giles?

What if the hunter who is after Angel is hunting him for a damn good reason, one no one could possibly argue with?

Angel did a lot of horrible things in the more than a century before he was cursed with the return of his soul. It only stands to reason that there might still be people, beings, entities out there who bear him a serious grudge for those actions.

Well . . . there isn't a whole lot more I can say about that without giving everything away. As an interesting note, though, I should point out that I've written before about how writers should never throw good ideas away because chances are you'll get a chance to use them eventually.

Tom and I had pitched an idea for an issue of the monthly *Angel* comic book called "The Fearless Vampire Killer," the title an homage to a classic B-movie. The story took place in the 1800s when Angel was the scourge of Europe. It was meant to be a stand-alone story illustrating just how unrepentantly evil our hero had been once upon a time. Unfortunately, the Powers That Be decided that they didn't want us to ever do a story in which Angel was shown only as his evil self. It was one thing, apparently, to acknowledge his past, but no one wanted to dwell on it.

We were pretty disappointed, I have to confess.

Then "Past Lives" came up. During our conversations, Tom and I realized that the story meant for "The Fearless Vampire Killer" was the final piece of the puzzle that would make this crossover event the kind of story we knew it could be. In our minds, it was the sort of thing that they would never be able to do on television, but that might happen if they ever decide to make that *Buffy* movie that has been rumored for so long.

Not *this* story, of course. But a story that includes all of your favorite characters and has a special-effects budget that would allow the producers to do whatever they wanted to do.

On that front, to give credit where credit is due, the demons in "Past Lives" are a little more inventive than you might have found in previous stories we've done for this mythos. That was Tom. He wanted to make sure they were different. I think he – and the art team – succeeded, but you'll have to be the judge of that.

Finally, since we're giving out credit, this story would not be nearly as effective were it not for the amazing efforts of the entire art team, particularly pencilers Cliff Richards and Christian Zanier, both of whom turned in some of their best work for "Past Lives." The character of Alexa Landry was staked out as the perfect territory for Christian to showcase his talents as a "Bad Girl" artist, which he had little opportunity to do in the regular *Angel* series. You'll see within what a stellar job he did with her design. When circumstances prevented Christian from drawing the entire crossover, Cliff Richards jumped in and did some absolutely wonderful work.

By now, you've probably guessed that Sniegoski and I had a lot of fun on this project.

We hope you do, too.

– Christopher Golden

WHATEVER HER INTENTIONS, SHE'S GOING TO GET ME KILLED IF I DON'T DO SOMETHING. WE'VE GOT TO FIND THIS WOMAN.

FIND HER AND PUT HER *OUT* OF BUSINESS, RIGHT? CUZ WE CAN'T AFFORD ANYONE ELSE ON THE PAYROLL.

WHOEVER SHE IS, SHE'S BEEN BUSY. FOR EVERY ONE THAT ATTACKS ME, I HAVE A FEELING SHE'S KILLED FOUR OR FIVE. HOPEFULLY SHE WON'T BE TOO DIFFICULT TO FIND.

CORDELIA AND I WILL GET TO WORK ON IT STRAIGHT AWAY. MEANWHILE PERHAPS YOU OUGHT TO LIE DOWN A BIT BEFORE GOING OUT AGAIN. GIVE YOURSELF A CHANCE TO HEAL.

NO TIME FOR REST. NOT WHEN I'VE GOT A LOT OF PISSED-OFF DEMONS OUT THERE WAITING TO GET A PIECE OF ME.

I DO WANT TO READ UP ON THAT YUVRATH DEMON. I WANT TO BE READY WHEN I RUN INTO IT AGAIN. MEANWHILE THE TWO OF YOU KEEP YOUR EYES OPEN.

IF THESE THINGS ARE COMING AFTER ME, I DON'T WANT YOU TWO GETTING CAUGHT IN THE CROSSFIRE.

LONDON, ENGLAND.

"YOUR EXPERIMENT SEEMS TO BE FAILING, MR. TRAVERS. MISS LANDRY HAS TALLIED AN IMPRESSIVE NUMBER OF KILLS OF LATE, BUT FAR TOO MANY HAVE ESCAPED."

"I WOULDN'T CALL THAT FAILURE. ALEXA LANDRY MAY HAVE BEEN GIVEN ACCESS TO A UNIQUE ARSENAL OF TOOLS FOR THE JOB...

"...BUT SHE IS NEVERTHELESS MERELY A PARTICULARLY TALENTED COUNCIL OPERATIVE. SHE IS *NOT* A SLAYER."

WE'RE WELL AWARE OF THAT, MR. TRAVERS, PAINFULLY SO. MISS LANDRY WAS AN EXEMPLARY OPERA- TIVE BEFORE THIS... EXPERIMENT BEGAN.

YES, BUT HER WORK OF LATE HAS BEEN SLOPPY. IN THE EYES OF THE INTER- NATIONAL SORCERY COMMUNITY, WE CANNOT AFFORD ANOTHER EMBARRASSMENT.

MY FRIENDS, I AM A MEMBER OF THIS BOARD, A COUNCIL DIRECTOR. AS WERE MY FATHER AND GRANDFATHER BEFORE ME. NO ONE CARES MORE ABOUT THE WELL-BEING OF THIS ORGANIZATION.

I WILL SPEAK TO MISS LANDRY IMMEDIATELY. IF IT SEEMS THE ONLY LOGICAL RECOURSE, I WILL RECALL HER TO LONDON AND RETURN HER TO HER FORMER DUTIES.

SEE THAT YOU DO, QUENTIN. SEE THAT YOU DO.

NO, SERIOUSLY, BUFF. HELP ME OUT.

WE KNOW HELLMOUTH IS TO DEMONS WHAT A DONUT SHOP IS TO COPS, RIGHT? BUT *HELLO?* SLAYER IN TOWN YOU'VE BEEN HERE LONG ENOUGH FOR THEM TO HAVE FIGURED IT OUT.

THAT SEXY HELLMOUTH GLOW? PRETTY MUCH THE DEADLY LURE OF THE BACKYARD BUG ZAPPER AS LONG AS YOU'RE AROUND. SO WHY DO THEY KEEP COMING?

WHAT CAN I SAY, XAND? MONSTERS. JUST NOT THAT BRIGHT.

ACTUALLY, SOME OF THEM ARE EXTREMELY INTELLIGENT. JUST, Y'KNOW, TOO FULL OF THEIR OWN DEMON-Y SELVES TO BE AFRAID.

FOR SOME, IT COULD BE THAT THE PULL OF THE HELLMOUTH IS SIMPLY STRONGER THAN THEIR FEAR. OTHERS... I JUST DON'T UNDER-STAND.

TELL ME ABOUT IT. I TOLD YOU GUYS ABOUT THE BONE-HEAD WITH THE SWORD THE OTHER DAY.

ON THE RUN FROM SOME DEMON HUNTER, SO HE COMES HERE? WE CAN SAFELY ASSUME *NOT* ON THE HONOR ROLL AT THE GHOUL SCHOOL.

"NO ONE KNOWS."

UCLA MEDICAL CENTER.

HER NAME'S ALEXA?

PARDON ME?

I HEARD YOU ON THE PHONE WITH GILES. THIS PSYCHO-WITCH WHO JUMPED US? HOW WELL DO YOU KNOW HER, WESLEY?

NOT NEARLY AS WELL AS GILES DOES. LAST I SAW HER, ALEXA LANDRY WAS A FIELD OPERATIVE FOR THE WATCHERS' COUNCIL.

BUT I CANNOT IMAGINE THAT HER ACTIONS HERE ARE ON THEIR BEHALF.

NOT THAT I WAS EAVESDROPPING, BUT HELLO? YOU AND THIS DEMON HUNTER CHICK USED TO HAVE A THING?

DON'T YOU EVER KNOCK?

WANT ME TO PRETEND I DIDN'T HEAR THAT?

FOR A BRIEF PERIOD, WHEN SHE FIRST BECAME AN OPERATIVE FOR THE COUNCIL, I WAS INDEED...INVOLVED WITH ALEXA LANDRY.

I BROKE IT OFF WHEN IT BECAME CLEAR TO ME THAT SHE ENJOYED THE MORE...VISCERAL ASPECTS OF HER DUTIES A BIT MORE THAN WAS HEALTHY, OR PROPER.

THE PAST ALWAYS COMES BACK TO HAUNT US.

INDEED.

R NAME IS ALEXA
NDRY. THE COUNCIL
WATCHERS MADE
R INTO THEIR
TIMATE OPERATIVE.

EY GAVE HER
ESS TO EVERY
GICAL WEAPON
THEIR ARSENAL,
VERY SECRET
ELL IN THEIR
OSSESSION.

WAS THE CHANCE
R WHICH SHE HAD
TED HER WHOLE LIFE.

UNGHHH!

YOU DON'T KNOW HOW I'VE DREAMED OF THIS MOMENT, ANGELLUS. YOU AT MY MERCY.

I'M NOT QUITE AT YOUR MERCY.

THE CHANCE FOR VENGEANCE.

TARA AND I HAVE SOME WITCHY *MISSION: IMPOSSIBLE* OR OTHER, 'CAUSE, YOU KNOW, OF THE MAGIC.

AND, XAND, SHE WANTS YOU AND ANYA TO LOOK OUT FOR WESLEY AND CORDELIA. IT'S PRETTY OBVIOUS THAT THIS WOMAN HAS MADE THEM TARGETS TOO.

AND... *RILEY?* I DIDN'T HEAR RILEY IN THERE.

RIGHT. WHICH WOULD BE BECAUSE BUFFY NEEDS SOMEONE TO HOLD DOWN THE FORT HERE, AND YOU'RE THE ONLY ONE SHE TRUSTS TO DO THAT. HOLD IT. THE FORT, I MEAN.

HAT'S RIDICU- OUS. I COULD OLD THE FORT. E'VE HELD THE ORT BEFORE. 'M GOOD WITH THE FORT.

XANDER, DON'T BE OBTUSE. BUFFY DOESN'T WANT RILEY TO COME TO LOS ANGELES BECAUSE SHE USED TO HAVE SEX WITH ANGEL, AND SHE HAS SEX WITH RILEY NOW.

GREAT. THANKS FOR CLEARING THAT UP, ANYA. REALLY.

THE LANDRY ESTATE, SHEFFIELD, GREAT BRITAIN.

1854.

THE FIRST TIME ANDREW LANDRY SAW A VAMPIRE HE WAS FOURTEEN YEARS OLD. HE HAS BEEN HUNTING THEM EVER SINCE.

THIRTEEN YEARS AGO, HIS QUEST WAS FOREVER ALTERED.

ANDREW LANDRY HAD THOUGHT HIMSELF A HERO, THEN.

BUT A HERO WOULD HAVE SAVED THEM.

HE HAD THOUGHT HIMSELF A PIOUS MAN.

BUT A PIOUS MAN, HAVING LOOKED THE DEVIL IN THE FACE, WOULD HAVE TURNED AWAY, PUT HIS FAITH IN GOD.

1845.

HE HAD THOUGHT HIMSELF A WISE MAN.

BUT A WISE MAN WOULD HAVE ABANDONED SO FOOLISH A QUEST, WOULD NEVER HAVE CONTINUED TO LEAD GOOD MEN TO THEIR DEATHS AT THE HANDS OF A FIEND FROM THE INFERNO ITSELF.

KNOCK KNOCK KNOCK

ENTER.

SIR ANDREW? MRS. LANDRY WOULD LIKE TO KNOW IF YOU WISH TO SEE YOUNG ALEX BEFORE HE GOES DOWN FOR THE NIGHT.

TO BE HONEST, SIR, I THINK SHE MAY ALSO HAVE BEEN A BIT CONCER FOR YOU. YOU HAVE BEEN LOCKED AW IN THERE FOR HOURS.

THERE ARE SOME THOUGHTS BETTER KEPT AWAY FROM A HAPPY FAMILY, ELIZABETH.

NOW RUN ALONG, DEAR. YOU HAD PLANNED TO MEET YOUR YOUNG MAN TONIGHT, I BELIEVE.

THANK YOU, SIR.

BUT HE'S ALREADY ARRIVED.

MARGARET? WHY IS IT DARK? IS THE LITTLE ONE ALREADY ASLEEP?

LOVELY PLACE YOU'VE GOT HERE, SIR ANDREW. AN ADORABLE FAMILY...

...AND THE MOST GULLIBLE SERVANTS.

YOUNG ELIZABETH THOUGHT I LOVED HER. CAN YOU IMAGINE?

HSSSSS

MARGARET, NO!

YOUR MUM AND DA ARE HAVING A WEE SPAT, LITTLE ALEX. NOTHING TO BE TROUBLED ABOUT.

ANGELUS! BY ALL THAT IS SACRED--

HEY. VISITING HOURS OVER YET, OR CAN I COME IN?

ANGEL! THANK THE LORD. WHEN WE HADN'T HEARD FROM YOU, WE THOUGHT THE WORST.

OR, AT LEAST, WE THOUGHT SIGOURNEY WEAVER HAD CAUGHT UP WITH YOU.

WHICH, GIVEN HOW CRAPPY YOU LOOK, WAS APPARENTLY NOT TOO FAR FROM THE TRUTH.

THANKS FOR THE VOTE OF CONFIDENCE, CORDELIA. AND I'M FINE, BY THE WAY. RELIEVED TO SEE THAT YOU TWO ARE IN ONE PIECE. MORE OR LESS.

NOW WE'VE JUST GOT TO FIGURE OUT WHO WE'RE DEALING WITH HERE.

ACTUALLY, ANGEL, WE ALREADY KNOW. SHE'S A COUNCIL OPERATIVE. THOUGH I'VE NO IDEA WHY SHE SEEMS TO HAVE FOCUSED HER ENERGIES ON YOU. HER NAME IS ALEXA LANDRY.

SHE'S A LANDRY?

NO WONDER SHE WANTS TO KILL ME.

THE PAST HAS COME BACK TO HAUNT ANGEL, BUFFY, AND GILES IN THE FORM OF ALEXA LANDRY, A WOMAN GIVEN ACCESS TO GREAT MAGICAL POWER BY THE COUNCIL OF WATCHERS, WHO WERE IGNORANT OF HER TRUE PURPOSE.

NOW HER MENTOR, QUENTIN TRAVERS, HAS PAID IN BLOOD FOR THAT IGNORANCE.

MR. TRAVERS MUST HAVE SECURITY AT ALL TIMES. HIS ATTACKER MIGHT RETURN AT ANY MOMENT. I SHALL CONTACT HIS EMPLOYERS. I'M SURE YOU'LL HEAR FROM THEM SOON ENOUGH.

LANDRY'S A NAME I HAVEN'T HEARD IN A LONG TIME, GILES. I KNOW WHY SHE'S AFTER ME. BUT WHAT'S HER CONNECTION TO THE REST OF YOU?

ALEXA HAS BEEN AN OPERATIVE OF THE COUNCIL FOR SOME YEARS, AND A MUCH TRUSTED ONE. TRUSTED TOO MUCH, IT SEEMS.

THEY TRAINED HER TO BE SOMETHING MORE, NEVER REALIZING SHE WAS MANIPULATING THEM ALL. I WARNED THEM YEARS AGO THAT SHE WAS TOO VOLATILE.

THEY ASSUMED IT WAS MERELY THE BITTERNESS OF A JILTED LOVER. WHO WOULD HAVE BELIEVED ME IF I HAD TOLD THEM I HAD BEEN THE ONE TO END THINGS?

OKAY, SO WE KNOW SHE'S NOT PRESIDENT OF THE GILES FAN CLUB. BUT WHY YOU, ANGEL? I SAW YOUR FACE WHEN YOU HEARD THIS WHACKO'S NAME. WHAT IS SHE TO YOU?

WHY DOES SHE HATE YOU SO MUCH?

Stake out these Buffy the Vampire Slayer and Angel trade paperbacks

Uninvited Guests

Ring of Fire

BAD BLOOD

DEMONS

Supernatural Defense Kit

PALE REFLECTIONS